This Book Belongs To:

The Muppet Babies live in a nursery
in a house on a street that is a lot like yours.
But they can travel anywhere anytime using a special power—
the power of the imagination.
Can you imagine what it would be like to go with them?
Join the Muppet Babies on this adventure and find out.

Weekly Reader Presents

Animal Go Bye-Bye

By Louise Gikow • Illustrated by Tom Brannon

Muppet Press/Marvel

This book is a presentation of
Weekly Reader Books.

Weekly Reader Books offers book clubs for children
from preschool through high school.

For further information write to:
Weekly Reader Books
4343 Equity Drive
Columbus, Ohio 43228

ISBN 0-87135-097-1

"Come on, Animal! Time for your nap."

Baby Kermit had called Baby Animal three times. But Animal wasn't paying any attention. He had a piece of paper in front of him, and he was busy drawing a picture of an amusement park.

"No sleep!" Animal shouted. "Animal go here!" And he pointed to his picture.

"No, Animal," said Kermit patiently. "You can't go to
the amusement park now. You have to take your nap."
"No nap!" Animal said stubbornly. "Animal go bye-bye!"

Animal shut his eyes tight. When he opened them, there was the Ferris wheel, and the merry-go-round, and best of all, there was the roller coaster.

"Animal go roller coaster!" he said happily, climbing in.

"Animal," said a voice behind him. Animal turned
around—and there was Kermit.

"It's time for your nap," Kermit said. "Come on!"

"No! Animal go bye-bye!"

When Animal got off the roller coaster, Kermit was still there.

"Submarine! Animal ride submarine!" Animal said.

"Nap! Animal take nap!" Kermit replied, looking a little angry.

"Submarine!"

"Nap!"

The submarine took Animal to a desert island.
"Animal play in sand!" Animal began throwing sand
around everywhere.

"Animal go nap!" Kermit said, popping up right behind him.

"No nap!" Animal shook his head. "Animal go bye-bye!"

Animal went out on deck.
"Animal play game!" he said.
"Animal sleep!" Kermit called out as he climbed aboard
the ship.

"No! Animal go bye-bye!" Animal jumped into a
lifeboat and rowed away.

Animal rowed for a long time. Finally, he reached the shore.

"Big building!" Animal said, looking up.

"Big trouble!" Kermit answered. "Animal, you'll be in big trouble if you don't take your nap."

"Animal go bye-bye," Animal said, waving.

From the top of the building, Animal could see the whole city.

"Animal look!" he cried.

"Animal sleep," Kermit said.

"Animal no sleep! Animal go bye-bye!"

The balloon took Animal off to a big airport.
Animal watched the jet planes take off and land.
"Animal fly away!" he said, jumping up and down.

"Animal," Kermit sighed. "If you don't take your nap, Nanny will be very angry."

"Animal go bye-bye!" Animal shouted.

Animal sat back and looked out the window of the airplane. He was a little tired after all his adventures. Soon, his eyes started to close.

"Animal sleepy," he murmured.

As he began to fall asleep, Animal felt the flight attendant covering him with a soft blanket. "Why don't you take a nice nap?" Animal heard him say.

Kermit finished covering Animal with the blanket.
Animal had already started to snore. But as Kermit
tiptoed away, Animal opened one eye.

"Animal go bye-bye?" he whispered.
"Animal go bye-bye," Kermit whispered back.   "Sweet dreams."